RUN, MELINA, RUN!

by Damian Harvey and Ben Scruton

W

FRANKLIN WATTS

LONDON•SYDNEY

Melina ran as fast as her feet would carry her. It was early morning and the streets of Athens were quiet … the perfect time for a race. As she reached the market place, the air filled with the smell of fresh fish and exotic spices. Melina had to dodge between the busy merchants who were beginning to set up their stalls.

Over her shoulder, Melina saw that a couple
of the boys were catching up with her. They were
bigger and older than Melina, but that
didn't bother her. She couldn't remember
the last time she'd lost a race and she wasn't
going to lose this one.

Up ahead, the temple at the top of the Acropolis towered above the city. Melina would have to reach the steps that led up to the temple first to win the race.

Turning a corner, she almost ran into a flock of goats. Instead of stopping, she jumped over one of the startled animals and kept on running.

Then at last, Melina could see the temple ahead.

A familiar voice called out to her:

"Run, Melina, run!" It was her big brother, Alexio.

He was waiting for her with a huge grin

on his face. "You've beaten them all again,"

he laughed.

CHAPTER 2

"I always beat them," boasted Melina, watching the other runners approaching.

"You must get it from me," Alexio said.

"Ha!" laughed Melina. "I bet I could beat you, too."

Before Alexio could reply, the other boys reached the finish. They were all huffing and puffing, trying to catch their breath.

"Hey!" cried one of the boys. "Look! It's Alexio." Everyone in Athens knew Melina's brother. Alexio was a great athlete and had won every running race at the last games in Olympia. The boys stood up and gathered round him, excitedly.

"Did you see us run?" they asked.

Alexio nodded. "Yes," he grinned. "And I saw my little sister beat you all."

"Now we know why she beats us," said one of the boys. "You're the fastest runner in the whole of Greece. Your sister must get her speed from you."

Alexio just smiled, but Melina scowled.

"I get my speed from my feet," she said,

"not from my brother. And one day I will beat

him too. Then I'll be an Olympic champion."

All of the boys laughed at this. They knew it

could never happen. Girls weren't allowed

to compete in the Olympic Games.

CHAPTER 3

As they walked back to their farm, Melina wanted to talk to Alexio, but the other boys wouldn't leave him alone.

"Tell us about your races," they insisted.

"Was the Temple of Zeus as fantastic as everyone says?" they asked.

"Do you think we will be great Olympic champions one day?" they wanted to know.

Alexio laughed and told them all tales of the Olympic Games. He even acted out winning his final race and told them how hard they would have to train if they wanted to compete.

Melina loved her brother but she couldn't help feeling a little jealous. Everyone treated him like a hero. They looked up to him and admired him. Mother and Father were very proud of Alexio, too.

People came to their farm and left gifts for him. They gave him fine clothes and food. He received invitations to sit in the best seats at the theatre. There was even a statue of Alexio at Olympia where the games were held. But that was many miles away and Melina had never seen it.

CHAPTER 4

They were almost back at their farm by the time the other boys left.

"It's not fair!" complained Melina, "I can beat them all. I should be allowed to compete in the games to show how good I am."

Alexio sighed. "You know that can never happen," he said. "Women aren't even allowed to watch the Olympic Games."

14

"Well, I still don't think it's fair," said Melina.

Alexio shook his head. "It is the law,

and that is that," he said, firmly.

"There must be something I can do to make

Mother and Father proud," said Melina.

"You can get married and have lots of children,"

said Alexio, with a grin. "That will make them

both proud."

Melina glared at her brother. "I want to run,"
she said. "I want to win a race and have my own
statue at Olympia, just like you."

"The Olympic Games are not just about winning
a race," Alexio explained. "They are to honour
the great god Zeus."

Melina didn't give up. "Well I want to honour Zeus, too," she said.

Alexio suddenly grinned. "That's it," he cried. "You can't honour Zeus, but you can honour his wife, Hera. The Heraean games also take place every four years," Alexio told her. "Luckily, they're happening this year. You could run in those, but I will have to talk with Mother and Father first."

CHAPTER 5

Melina's parents weren't happy.

"It's a long way from here to Olympia,"
said Mother.

"Don't worry," said Grandpa Hector. "I will take
them to Olympia. Alexio and I will look after her."

"Girls from Athens never win," said Father,
shaking his head. "The girls from Sparta are
strong. They win everything."

"That's true," Alexio agreed. "But Melina is fast. Just think how proud you will be when she beats them all."

Father thought for a moment, then he nodded and smiled. "Go on then, Melina. Run!"

19

Mother was right, it was far away. It took four days to get to Olympia riding in Grandpa Hector's cart. Sitting with the other athletes, Melina realised her Father had been right, too.

The girls from Sparta were so much bigger than her. They looked down on Melina and laughed.

"You will never beat us," they said.

Melina was worried. Perhaps they were right.

Perhaps she didn't have a chance.

When Melina saw the crowds of people that had come to watch, she felt even worse. People were shouting and cheering for the Spartan athletes. Melina began to think that she should have stayed at home after all.

When the race started, the other runners sped ahead, quickly leaving Melina behind. They were tall and strong, and the crowd roared and cheered them on.

23

Melina tried her best to catch up, but it seemed useless. The other girls were bigger and faster than her and she was beginning to feel tired. Running in the games was much harder than she had ever dreamed it would be. Then she remembered how easily she beat all of the boys back home, even though they were bigger and older than her.

As she ran, Melina closed her eyes for a moment and imagined she was running through the streets of Athens. Then, above the roar of the crowd she heard Alexio and her Grandpa shouting: "Run Melina, run!"

It was just the thing that Melina needed.
The other athletes were big, but Melina knew
she was fast. She ran as fast as she could,
passing first one runner, then another and another.

Over the roar of the crowd, Melina was sure she
could still hear Alexio and her Grandpa shouting
her name, but now it seemed
as though more people
had joined them.

As she crossed the finish line in first place,
everyone was cheering her name.

"Melina! Melina! Melina!" they cried.

Alexio lifted Melina up onto his shoulders
and they walked past the cheering crowds.

Things to think about

1. Why does Melina feel jealous of her brother?
2. What idea does Alexio have that can help Melina?
3. What things were girls expected to do in ancient Greek times?
4. How does Melina feel during the big race? Is it what she expected?
5. Who did Melina depend on for help and support? How did they help her?

Write it yourself

One of the themes in this story is following your ambition. Now try to write your own story with a similar theme. Plan your story before you begin to write it.
Start off with a story map:

• a beginning to introduce the characters and where and when your story is set (the setting);
• a problem that the main characters will need to fix in the story;
• an ending where the problems are resolved.

Get writing! Try to add some dramatic or unpredicatable events in your story to keep your readers guessing how it will end. Use language with expression and exclamation!

Notes for parents and carers

Independent reading
The aim of independent reading is to read this book with ease. This series is designed to provide an opportunity for your child to read for pleasure and enjoyment. These notes are written for you to help your child make the most of this book.

About the book
Melina longs to compete in a running race at the Olympics, but only boys can take part in the race. Then her brother Alexio remembers that girls can compete in the Heraean games ... and so Melina enters the race of her life!

Before reading
Ask your child why they have selected this book. Look at the title and blurb together. What do they think it will be about? Do they think they will like it?

During reading
Encourage your child to read independently. If they get stuck on a longer word, remind them that they can find syllable chunks that can be sounded out from left to right. They can also read on in the sentence and think about what would make sense.

After reading
Support comprehension by talking about the story. What happened?
Then help your child think about the messages in the book that go beyond the story, using the questions on the page opposite. Give your child a chance to respond to the story, asking:
Did you enjoy the story and why? Who was your favourite character?
What was your favourite part? What did you expect to happen at the end?

Franklin Watts
First published in Great Britain in 2018
by The Watts Publishing Group

Series Editors: Jackie Hamley and Melanie Palmer
Series Advisors: Dr Sue Bodman and Glen Franklin
Series Designer: Peter Scoulding

A CIP catalogue record for this book is
available from the British Library.

ISBN 978 1 4451 6332 1 (hbk)
ISBN 978 1 4451 6334 5 (pbk)
ISBN 978 1 4451 6333 8 (library ebook)

Printed in China

Franklin Watts
An imprint of
Hachette Children's Group
Part of The Watts Publishing Group
Carmelite House
50 Victoria Embankment
London EC4Y 0DZ

An Hachette UK Company
www.hachette.co.uk

www.franklinwatts.co.uk

FSC
www.fsc.org
MIX
Paper from
responsible sources
FSC® C104740